D0505142

Essex County Council
3013021365110 1

DINOS

Sea monsters
tall monsters
Furry monsters

To my mum with all my love – C.F.

To Victoria, for being there every time I need a friend – C.R.

DON'T WAKE

First published in 2017
by Scholastic Children's Books Euston House, 24 Eversholt Street, London NW1 1DB
a division of Scholastic Ltd
www.scholastic.co.uk

London ~ New York ~ Toronto ~ Sydney ~ Auckland ~ Mexico City ~ New Delhi ~ Hong Kong
PB ISBN 978 1407 16722 0

1 3 5 7 9 10 8 6 4 2

Papers used by Scholastic Children's Books are made from wood grown in sustainable forests.

THE YETI

CLAIRE FREEDMAN
CLAUDIA RANUCCI

SCHOLASTIC

If you think there's a **yeti** curled under your bed,
Don't scream or panic. Don't lose your head.
As **yetis**, you know, are most **terribly** rare,

First check that it's not
something else hiding there.

Like those **polar bear slippers**
you kicked on the floor,

Or the **duvet** that Mum
couldn't fit in the drawer.

Oh dear, so you've checked,
and it couldn't be **that**,
And the furry white mound
is **too huge** for a **cat**.

Oh yikes – it's a yeti
– but phew, there's good news:
Those loud snuffly snores mean he's having a snooze.
You've now time to think of what action to take.

STOP! What are you doing?
Don't poke him awake!

You've given your yeti a fright – that's not right.
Tell him **you're sorry**, say humans don't bite!

BUT if he still finds your lampshade appealing,
Show him it's safe to come down from the ceiling.

Great! Now you're friends. GRRRRR! Is his tummy **growling?**

Quick!
Time to feed him,
before he starts howling.

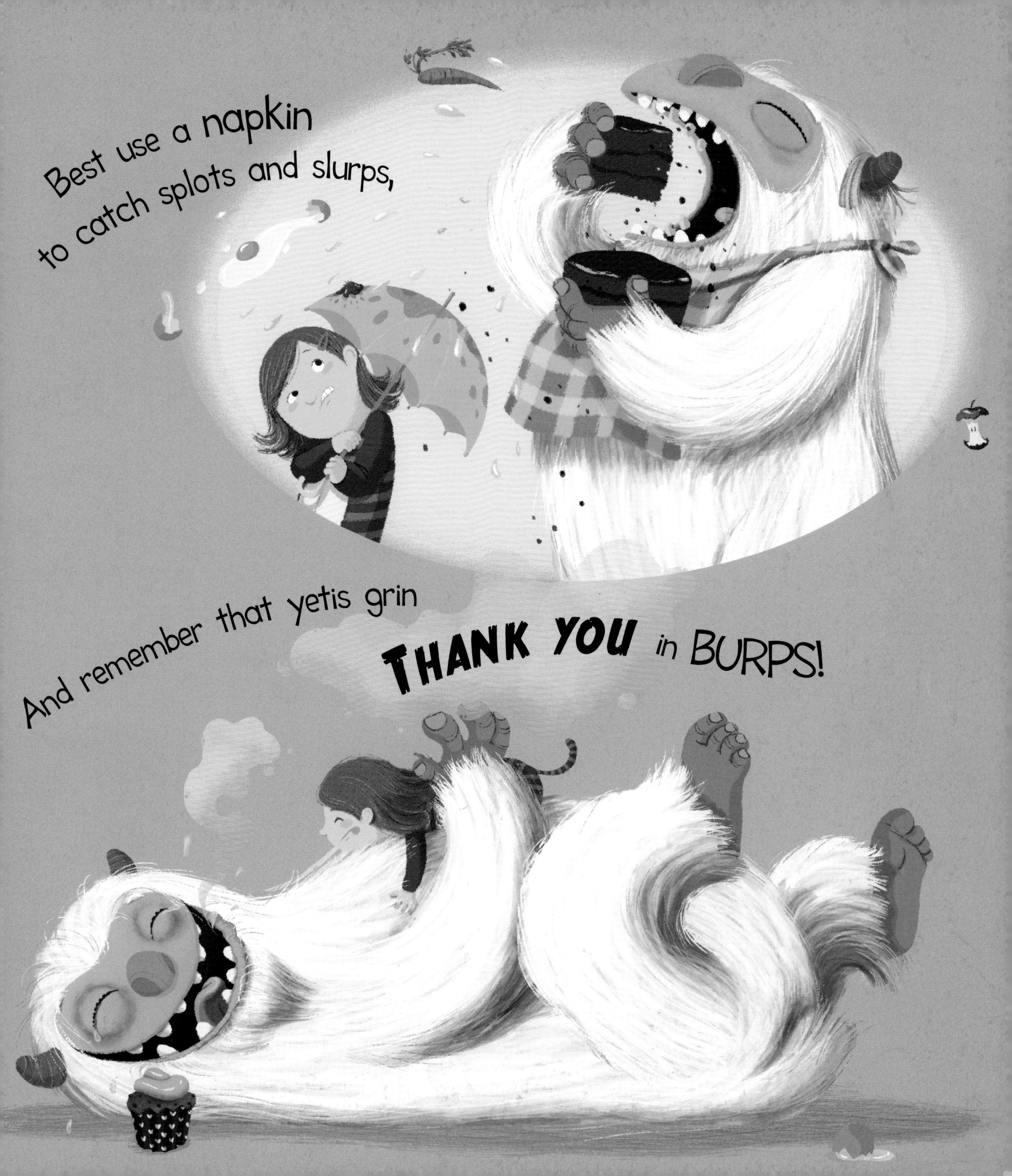
Best use a napkin
to catch splots and slurps,
And remember that yetis grin
THANK YOU in BURPS!

After you've cleaned up, he'll need a COLD bath.
He'll wear your mum's **bath-hat**, it's kind not to laugh.

Top up with ice cubes,
but don't even try
To stay in the room
when he shakes himself dry.

Of course, you'll be shouting,

He'll **beg** to go with you, your brand new **classmate.**

The teacher might think he's your "bring and show" pet –
Your friends will gasp, "WOW! He's the funniest yet!"

He'll eat all the slugs
on the playground – Ugh!
Yuck!
And don't let him loose on the slide – he'll get stuck!

He'll make loud
embarrassing noises –
Phooh-eeee!
But, always polite, he'll grin,
"Oops, pardon me!"

You should be aware – if you take Yeti shopping,
He'll **munch** all the food till his tummy is popping,

Then squeeze in the freezer (as yetis love snow)

And make a great fuss when you say, "Time to go!"

All yetis, unfortunately,
have TONS of fleas –
They tickle his tummy,
and big knobbly knees.

He'll ask you to scratch him
for itchy relief.
Take note! If he eats some,
you MUST brush his teeth.

By now you'll be asking,
"Help! What will Mum say?"
"A huge hairy yeti –
he can't stay! No way!"

The **fact** is that yetis
are great at **disguise.**

He's a **chair,**

then a **rug** –

in a **flash** of Mum's eyes.

Though keeping a yeti won't suit everyone,
They're cuddly and silly,
they're friendly and fun.

And things could be MUCH worse,
if under your bed...

You find a...

...huge Dinosaur
hiding instead!

DINOS

Sea monsters
tall monsters
Furry monsters